FROZEN IN TIME

Dear Reader

In my research for this book I found that 20 000 years ago humans were hunter-gatherers. They hunted animals and gathered plants, rather than farming for food.

Then, 10 000 years ago, the climate became warmer and wetter. People began to farm food for themselves. This change signalled the beginning of civilisation.

> MOST SCIENTISTS AGREE THAT EARTH'S CLIMATE IS CHANGING. BUT THEY MAY NOT AGREE ABOUT THE CAUSE ...

Now, we're faced with another change: Earth's climate is becoming even warmer. Imagine if YOU found a way to do something that could change the way we lived in this world.

People have changed before – we just need to think differently and we can change again!

John Parsons

NELSON
CENGAGE Learning™
For learning solutions, visit **cengage.com.au**

Contents

FROZEN IN TIME

page 12

3 Climate and People

Read about why early humans moved to new lands and how they adapted to new climates.

page 20

4 Lessons from the Past

If we learn about past climate changes, we can think of new ways to adapt to future climate change.

Why Is Our Climate Changing?

Is Earth **Slowly** Warming Up?

Many people around the world are concerned about the effects of climate change on our environment.

Most scientists agree that the climate of Earth is changing. But they may not agree about the cause.

GLOBAL WARMING

This term is used to describe the increase in the temperature of Earth's atmosphere.

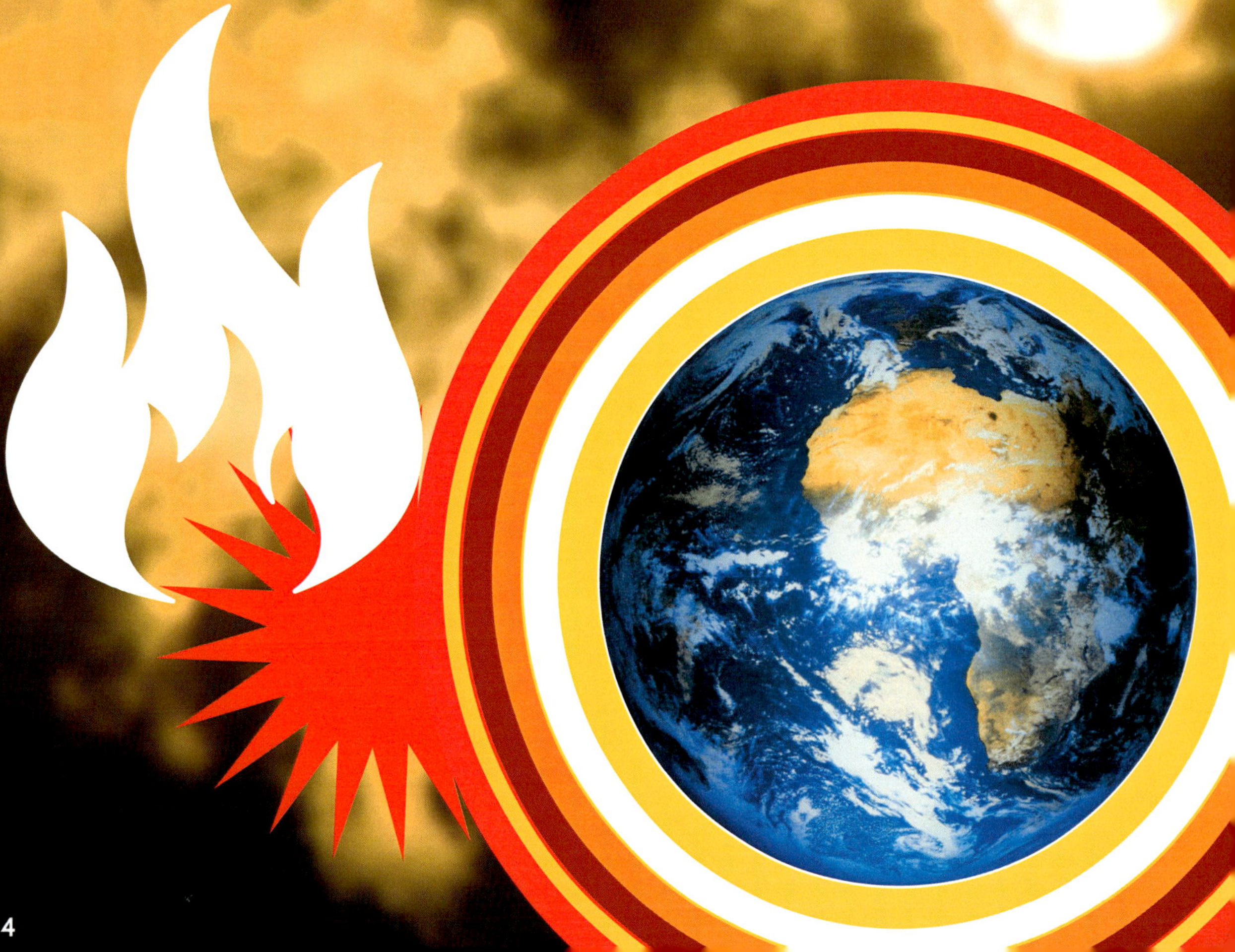

Scientific Viewpoint 1: Humans Cause Global Warming

Many scientists agree that global warming is caused by human activities, such as burning oil and coal, pollution and cutting down trees for farming. These activities increase greenhouse gases, like carbon dioxide and methane. Greenhouse gases act like a blanket around Earth. They stop heat escaping into space. Slowly, Earth warms up.

Global warming makes forests drier, which can lead to bushfires.

A logging truck carries away felled trees.

An oil refinery pollutes the air.

Cars release pollutants, such as carbon dioxide, into the air.

Scientific Viewpoint 2: Earth's Natural Climate Change Causes Global Warming

Some scientists argue that climate change is natural, and that Earth has been through several dramatic climate changes throughout its history.

Ice ages are one kind of natural climate change on Earth.

Earth Science

What Is an Ice Age?

An ice age is a period of time in which thick sheets of ice (or glaciers) cover large amounts of land. An ice age can last for millions of years.

By studying ice drilled from polar caps, scientists discovered that Earth had gone through several ice ages. They also found that each ice age had been followed by a warm, tropical period.

Life Science

Tree Growth Rings

Studying growth rings in very old trees is a technique that scientists use to study changes in Earth's climate. Trees grow faster in warm, wet conditions.

Tree rings show different growth rates.

The Climate Change Debate Continues

What do you think?

There is a lot of debate about what causes climate change, and whether or not we can slow it down. But there is little debate that the climate is changing.

Humans like us have been around for about 200 000 years. This is not the first time our species has had to adapt to dramatic changes in our environment.

Perhaps it would be wise for humans to look to the past for answers about how to prepare for a different climate in the future.

2 Are We Still in an Ice Age?

Climate Change Explained

Earth's history has seen a series of ice ages followed by warmer periods. This is a natural process and nothing to be alarmed about. Earth's climate changes from warm to cold for many reasons. Here are just a few.

TEXT TYPE
Exposition

1 Changes in Earth's Orbit

Orbiting closer to the Sun means warmer temperatures for the planet. Orbiting further away from the Sun brings about colder temperatures.

SUN

a warmer Earth, orbiting closer to the Sun

a cooler Earth, orbiting further from the Sun

SUN

2

Volcanic Activity

A rise in volcanic activity can increase the temperature on Earth. Less volcanic activity may result in a lower temperature.

3

Movement of the Oceans

Ocean currents can move warm and cold water around Earth. Changes in currents can change global temperatures.

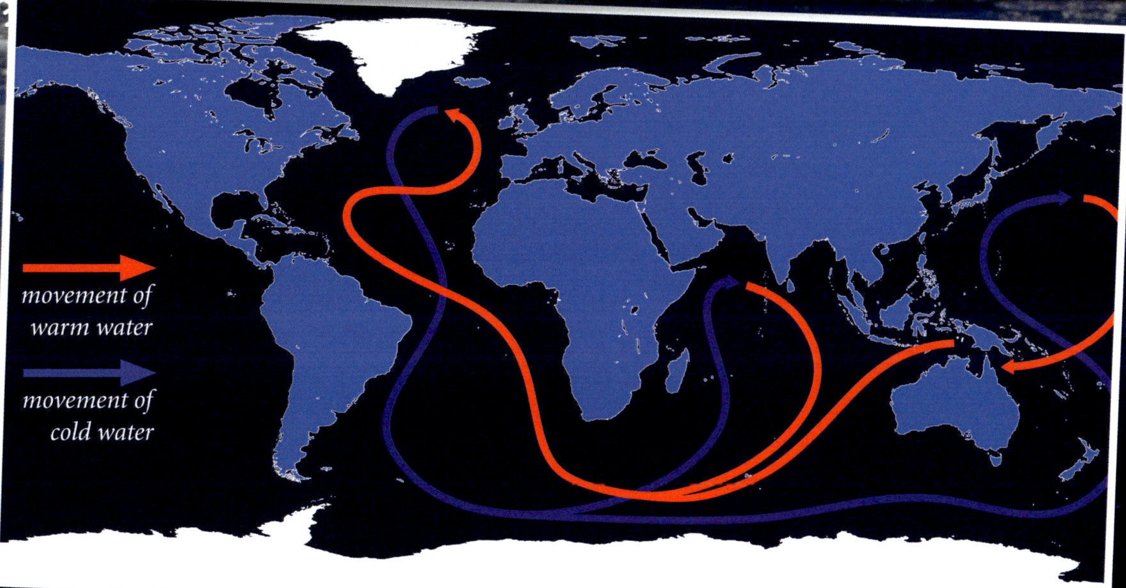

Ice Age Evidence

An ice age is a period of cooling, when temperatures get so cold that large amounts of water from oceans and lakes freeze up. Big ice sheets cover the land and sea. So much water is turned into ice that sea levels drop.

Even during these ice ages, there can be warm periods. When an ice age finishes, the frozen ice sheets melt and shrink. They release huge amounts of water. This causes the ocean levels to rise again.

There's a lot of evidence supporting our chapter topic: **Are We Still in an Ice Age?** What do you think?

leaf fossil on rock

Fossil Evidence

Fossils and geological studies show that Earth gets really cold every 40 000 years and every 100 000 years – but that it warms up in between those times.

Scientific Evidence

Scientific evidence proves that it is natural for Earth's climate to go through very cold and very warm periods. The sea levels and temperatures rise and fall during these periods, too. In fact, if this did not happen, we really would have something to worry about!

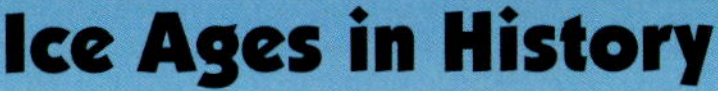

Ice Ages in History

1

The first ice age started around **2.7 billion years ago** and finished about 2.3 billion years ago.

2

The second ice age started around **850 million years ago** and finished about 630 million years ago.

3

The third ice age started **460 million years ago** and finished 430 million years ago.

4

The latest ice age started **2.6 million years ago**. It reached its peak only 20000 years ago. Climate scientists tell us we're still in this ice age.

New Lands, New Climates

Most scientists agree that the earliest humans like us lived in Africa around **200 000 years ago**. Africa would have been relatively warm, but the rest of the world was still in the middle of an ice age. Archaeologists tell us that humans started to move out of Africa around **100 000 years ago**.

Volcanic Ash Affected Earth's Climate

About **70 000 years ago** a volcanic eruption far away in Indonesia shot so much ash into the atmosphere that the sunshine was blocked. Earth's air temperature might have dropped by 3.5 degrees Celsius. Plants and animals would have died, and many people would have starved. In fact, humans nearly became extinct. Survivors would have had to travel long distances in search of food and water and better places to live.

a young Masai from the Masai Mara National Reserve, Kenya

The sun sets in Africa.

Earth Science

Volcanic Ash

After it settles, volcanic ash forms layers on the ground. Geologists use these lines of ash to date other objects found above or below the ash lines.

a volcanic eruption

ash lines in a road cutting

New, **Colder** Lands

When early humans moved to different lands, they would have experienced many different climates.

Keeping warm in cooler climates may have been a reason for early humans to first begin to wear clothing.

a modern image of what a female Neanderthal might have worn

Neanderthals became extinct about 30 000 years ago.

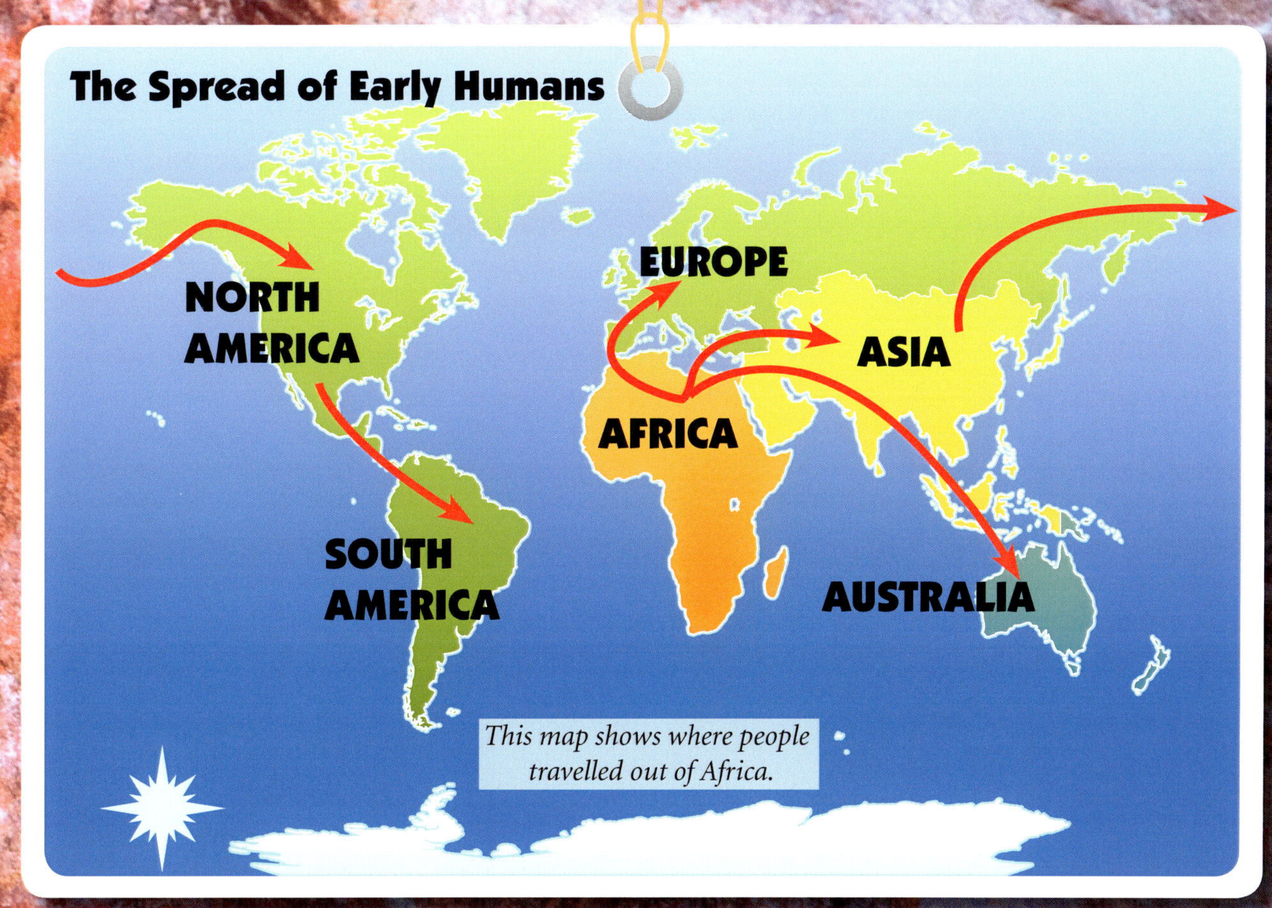

This map shows where people travelled out of Africa.

Still Cold!

Archaeologists think that humans like us were living in Europe, Asia and Australia by at least **40 000 years ago**. They would have had to work together just to survive. Food, clothing and shelter would have been difficult to find during that ice age.

At that time, there still would have been **20 000 years** of cold temperatures to come.

Will we have another 20 000 years of cold temperatures?

Walked **Across** the **Sea**

Humans arrived in North America around **15 000 years ago**. At that time, there was still so much ice around that sea levels were low. The first humans could have walked across what is now the Bering Sea, from the Asian continent to the North American continent.

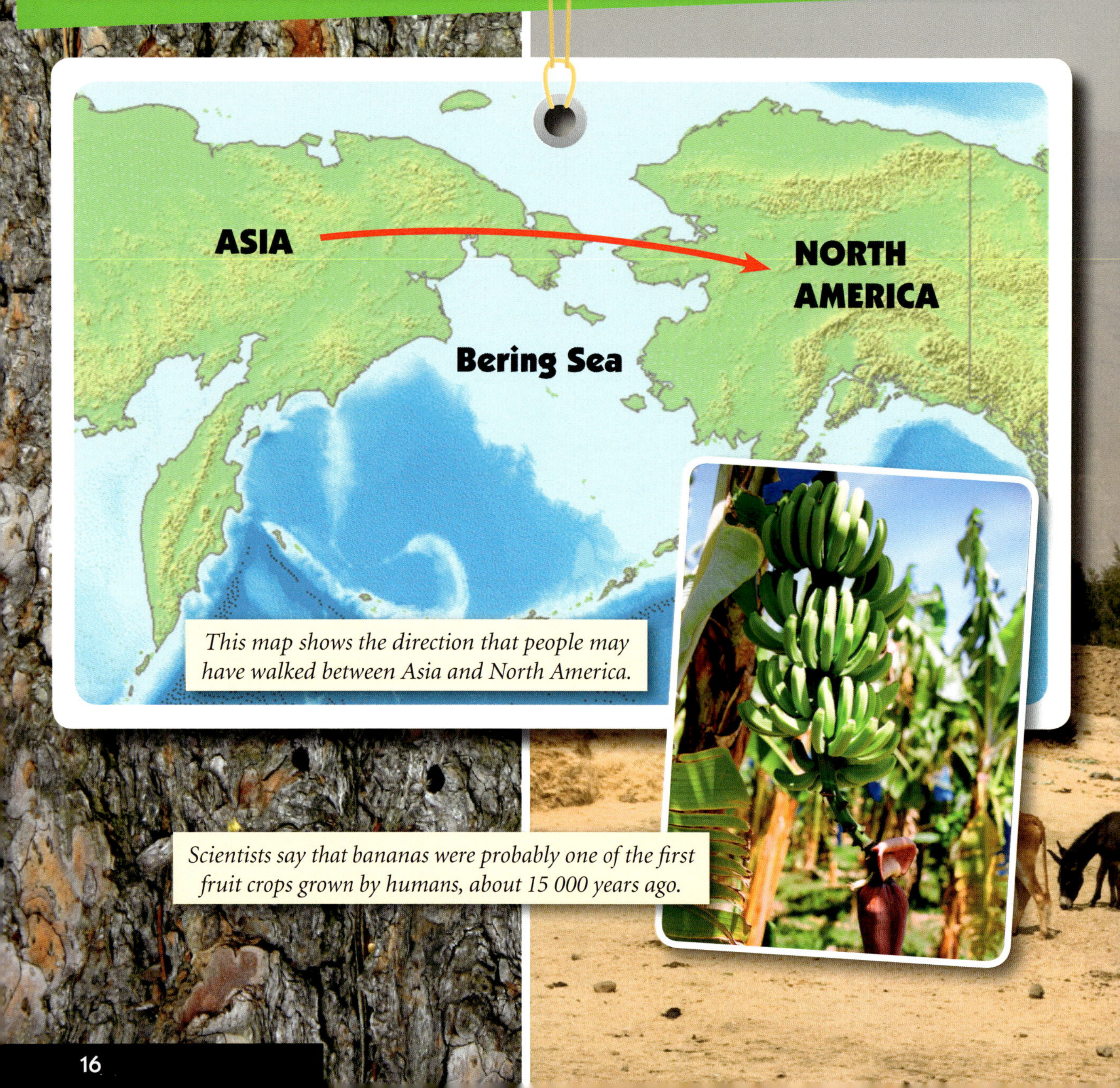

This map shows the direction that people may have walked between Asia and North America.

Scientists say that bananas were probably one of the first fruit crops grown by humans, about 15 000 years ago.

an Indian village with crops

harvested grains, spices, beans, nuts, fruit and herbs

The Climate Warms Up for Civilisation

Then, after the coldest part of the ice age, temperatures rose again. Glaciers started to shrink about **12 000 years ago**, and Earth's climate became warmer.

In some places on Earth people could grow enough food to settle in one place. It was the start of what we call civilisation.

The Start of **Farming**

When the worst of the ice age was over, and the world warmed up about **10 000 years ago**, more humans in many different places around the world changed from hunter-gatherers to farmers. Many groups learnt how to plant crops and tend animals.

food crops

sheep grazing

Social Studies

Who Were Hunter-Gatherers?

People were known as hunter-gatherers before they grew crops and raised animals. As hunters and gatherers they mostly gathered edible plants and took meat from dead animals in the wild. They hunted animals only when it was necessary.

images of hunters carved into rock

Climate Has Changed the Way People Live

Up until that time people had lived in small groups and were more or less equal. Once they settled and began to farm and store food, the size of the groups grew. Some became wealthy and powerful. With enough food for everyone, some people were free to spend time developing skills, such as pottery and weaving.

It seems that climate change has forced people to explore new ways of living. It has made us think about, learn and value new skills.

4 Lessons from the Past

People **Can** Change!

Can we learn from the past?

Many people have strong views about who – or what – is causing the changes to our climate. But one thing seems to be certain. The world we live in will change, just as it has in past times. It seems likely we will need to change, too, if we are to survive.

Perhaps the lessons we can learn from past climate change patterns could be valuable again.

Social Studies

Al Gore, Climate Change Activist

Al Gore was the USA's vice president from 1993 to 2001. Since leaving office, he has actively discussed issues relating to the climate change crisis around the world. His website keeps people informed about topics, such as sustainable living, climate change issues and clean energy sources. He is most famous for his book, An Inconvenient Truth: The Planetary Emergency of Global Warming and What We Can Do About It. *A movie called* An Inconvenient Truth *was released in 2006.*

Al Gore

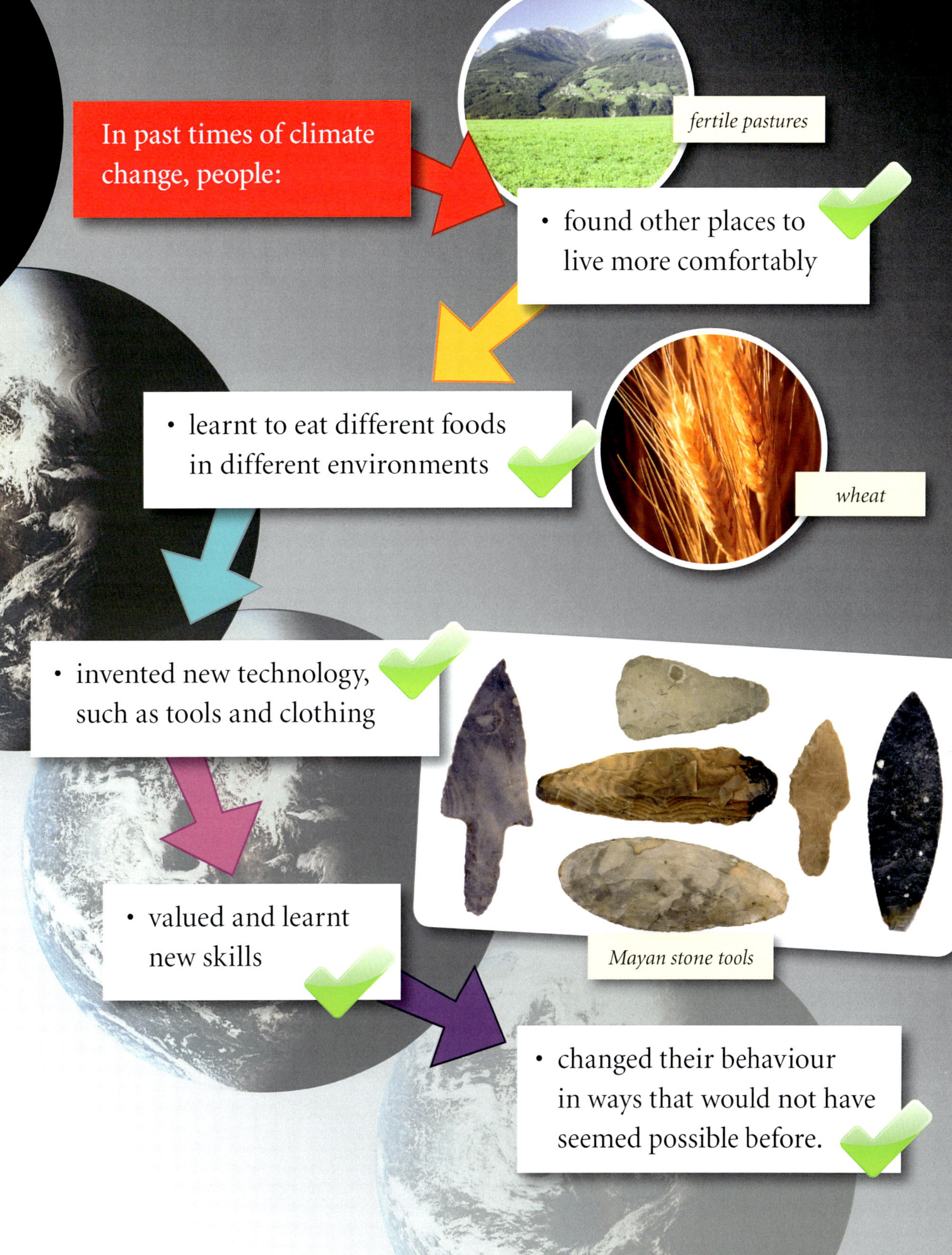
In past times of climate change, people:
fertile pastures
• found other places to live more comfortably
• learnt to eat different foods in different environments
wheat
• invented new technology, such as tools and clothing
• valued and learnt new skills
Mayan stone tools
• changed their behaviour in ways that would not have seemed possible before.

What's **Next** for Us?

Throughout history, the warmer climate helped people to change from hunter-gatherers to farmers. As we are now faced with the threat of global warming, many people are rethinking the way they live.

Maybe this is our opportunity to think about new ways to live within our environment. It may also be an opportunity to think about what we really value in life.

our flora and fauna

our ancient wonders

our frozen wonderlands

our atmosphere

our magnificent oceans

our natural wonders

Climate Change in Our Hands

Maybe if we look at the changes people have made in the past, and the ways they have had to learn to live differently, we can begin to understand the changes we will need to make in the future.

Changes for the Future

People may disagree about how things should change, but it is important to start thinking and talking about it before it is too late. Climate change is upon us – and this time it will be much faster, and we won't have 10 000 years to adapt.

our diverse cultures

our beautiful wildlife

Index

Glossary

archaeologists	Scientists who study past human societies and cultures using objects or evidence those people left behind
carbon dioxide	A gas that forms about 0.04 per cent of Earth's atmosphere, and that can prevent heat escaping into space
geologists	Scientists who study Earth and the materials that it is made of, such as rocks
Mayan	A culture and society that existed in Central America from 2000 BCE until the 1600s
methane	A gas that can be formed by burning or consuming organic materials, such as plants, coal and oil
Neanderthal	The name given to early human-like creatures that lived between 130 000 to 30 000 years ago
polar caps	The areas of ice that exist in the regions of Earth's North Pole and South Pole
sustainable living	A way of living that does not use up food, fuel, minerals or other resources that cannot be replaced